This Book Belongs To:

Read to Me Grandpa

Stories, songs and rhymes for you to enjoy together

This is a Dempsey Parr Book
First published in 2000
Dempsey Parr is an imprint of Parragon
Parragon, Queen Street House, 4 Queen Street, Bath BA1 1HE, UK

Produced by The Templar Company plc,
Pippbrook Mill, London Road, Dorking, Surrey RH4 1JE, UK

Compiled and edited by Caroline Repchuk
Designed by Kilnwood Graphics

Printed and bound in Spain
ISBN 1-84084-943-6

Read to Me Grandpa

Stories, songs and rhymes for you to enjoy together

DP
DEMPSEY
PARR

Contents

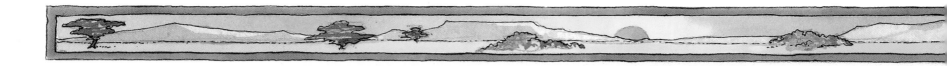

Action Songs

A collection of
traditional action
songs with easy
to follow pictures
to show you
what to do.

Five Little Soldiers

Five little soldiers standing in a row,
Three stood straight,

And two stood — so.
Along came the captain,
And what do you think?
They ALL stood straight,
As quick as a wink.

Hold five fingers up

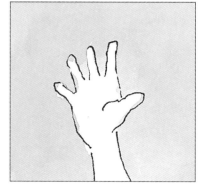

FIVE LITTLE SOLDIERS

Fold down two fingers

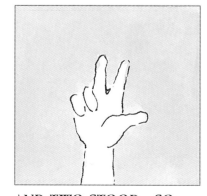

AND TWO STOOD - SO

Pass index finger of other hand in front

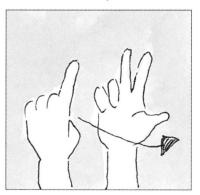

...WHAT DO YOU THINK

Straighten all fingers

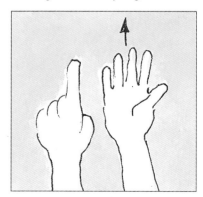

...ALL STOOD STRAIGHT

Here Sits the Lord Mayor

Here sits the Lord Mayor,

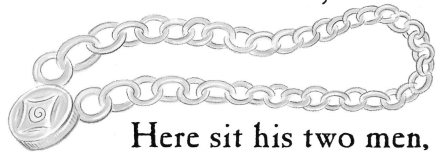

Here sit his two men,

Here sits the cocky,

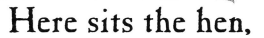

Here sits the hen,

Here sit the chicks,

And here they run in,

Chin chopper,
chin chopper,
chin chopper,
chin.

Row, Row, Row Your Boat

Row, row, row your boat,
Gently down the stream,
Merrily, merrily, merrily, merrily,
Life is but a dream.

Mime rowing action throughout...

Round About There

Round about there,
Sat a little hare,
A cat came and
chased him,
Right up there!

Circle child's palm with finger

ROUND ABOUT THERE

Walk fingers up arm

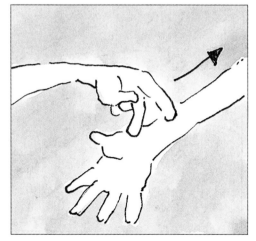

A CAT CAME AND CHASED HIM

Tickle!

RIGHT UP THERE!

The Wheels on the Bus

The wheels on the bus go round and round,
Round and round, round and round,
The wheels on the bus
go round and round,
All day long.

The wipers on
the bus go swish,
swish, swish, etc.

The horn on the bus
goes beep! beep! beep! etc.

*Move fists in a
circular motion*

ROUND AND ROUND

*Waggle both extended
index fingers*

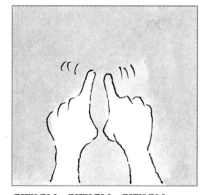

SWISH, SWISH, SWISH

Pretend to press a horn

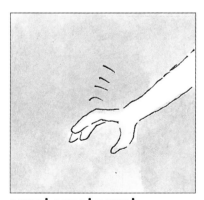

BEEP! BEEP! BEEP!

*Pat thumb on rest of
extended fingers*

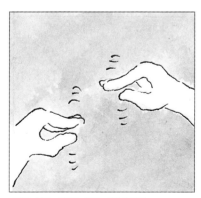

CHAT, CHAT, CHAT

The people on the bus go chat, chat, chat, etc.

The children on the bus bump up and down, etc.

The babies on
the bus go "WAAH!
WAAH! WAAH!", etc.

The grannies on
the bus go knit,
knit, knit, etc.

The wheels on
the bus go round
and round,
All day long.

*Bump up and
down on chair*

BUMP UP AND DOWN

*Make 'waah' sound with
hands around mouth*

WAAH! WAAH! WAAH!

*Pretend to knit with
extended index fingers*

KNIT, KNIT, KNIT

Repeat first action

ROUND AND ROUND

Two Little Men in a Flying Saucer

Move arms up and down

Lift baby in circle

Two little men in a flying saucer
Flew round the world one day.

They looked to the left and right a bit,
And couldn't bear the sight of it,

And then they flew away.

Turn head left

Turn head right

Cover eyes

Repeat first action

Tall Shop

Raise arms above head

Tall shop in the town.

Swing forearms open and shut

Doors swinging round about.

Move hands up and down

Lifts moving up and down.

Move fists back and forth

People moving in and out.

I Hear Thunder

(To the tune of Frère Jacques)

I hear thunder,
I hear thunder,
Oh! Don't you?
Oh! Don't you?

Pitter, patter raindrops,
Pitter, patter raindrops,
I'm wet through,
I'm wet through.

Pretend to listen

I HEAR THUNDER

Flutter hands like rain

PITTER, PATTER RAINDROPS

Wrap arms around body

I'M WET THROUGH

Hurry up the sunshine,
Hurry up the sunshine,
I'll soon dry,
I'll soon dry.

I see blue skies,
I see blue skies,
Way up high,
Way up high.

Point up to sky

WAY UP HIGH

Circle hands in front of chest

HURRY UP THE SUNSHINE

Pretend to shake hands dry

I'LL SOON DRY

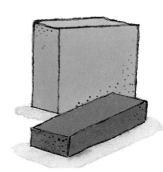

Build a House with Five Bricks

Build a house with five bricks,
One, two, three, four, five.

Make a roof

Put a roof on top,

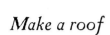

And a chimney too,

Blow!

Where the wind
blows through!

Knock at the Door

Knock on forehead

Knock at the door,

Lift eyebrow

Peep in,

Pull ear

Ring the bell,

Push nose up

Lift the latch,

Put finger in mouth

And walk in.

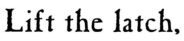

23

Five Fat Sausages

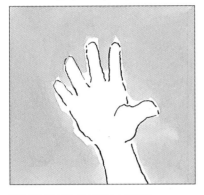

Hold up five fingers

FIVE FAT SAUSAGES

Clap!

...ONE WENT BANG!

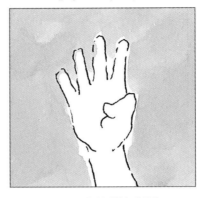

Hold up four fingers

FOUR FAT SAUSAGES

Clap!

...ONE WENT BANG!

Five fat sausages frying in a pan,
All of a sudden one went 'BANG!'
Four fat sausages, etc.
Three fat sausages, etc.
Two fat sausages, etc.
One fat sausage frying in a pan,
All of a sudden it went 'BANG!'
and there were NO sausages left!

Continue until one finger left

ONE FAT SAUSAGE

Clap!

...IT WENT BANG!

NO SAUSAGES!

Two Fat Gentlemen

Two fat gentlemen
met in a lane,
Bowed most politely,
bowed once again.
How do you do?
How do you do?
How do you do again?

Two thin ladies met in a lane, etc.
Two tall policemen met in a lane, etc.
Two little schoolboys met in a lane, etc.
Two little babies met in a lane, etc.

Repeat actions for other fingers: two thin ladies = index fingers, etc.

*Hold out fists
with thumbs raised*

Bend each thumb in turn

*Wiggle each
thumb in turn*

Wiggle thumbs together

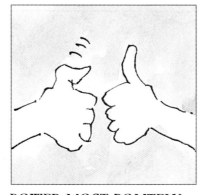

TWO FAT GENTLEMEN

BOWED MOST POLITELY

HOW DO YOU DO?

HOW DO YOU DO AGAIN?

Ten Little Fingers

I have ten little fingers,
And they all belong to me.
I can make them do things,

Would you like to see?
I can shut them up tight,
Or open them all wide.

Hold hands up

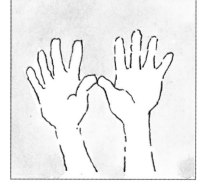

TEN LITTLE FINGERS

Waggle fingers

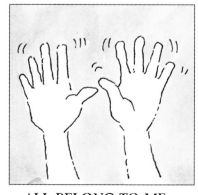

...ALL BELONG TO ME...

Clench fists

...SHUT THEM TIGHT...

Open hands wide

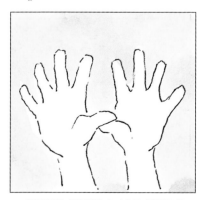

...OPEN THEM ALL WIDE

Put them all together,
Or make them all hide.
I can make them jump high;

I can make them jump low.
I can fold them quietly,
And hold them all just so.

Interlock fingers

PUT THEM ALTOGETHER

Place hands behind back

...MAKE THEM ALL HIDE...

Move arms up and down

...JUMP HIGH/LOW...

Put hands together in lap

HOLD THEM ALL JUST SO

I Am A Music Man

LEADER: I am a music man,
            I come from far away,
            And I can play.
ALL: What can you play?
LEADER: I play piano.
ALL: Pia, pia, piano, piano, piano,
            Pia, pia, piano, pia, piano.

LEADER: I am a music man,
            I come from far away,
            And I can play.
ALL: What can you play?
LEADER: I play the big drum.
ALL: Boomdi, boomdi, boomdi boom,
            Boomdi boom, boomdi boom,
            Boomdi, boomdi, boomdi boom,
            Boomdi, boomdi boom.
            Pia, pia, piano, piano, piano,
            Pia, pia, piano, pia, piano.

28

LEADER: I am a music man,
I come from far away,
And I can play.

ALL: What can you play?

LEADER: I play the trumpet.

ALL: Tooti, tooti, tooti, toot,
Tooti, toot, tooti, toot,
Tooti, tooti, tooti, toot,
Tooti, tooti, toot.

Boomdi, boomdi, boomdi boom,
Boomdi boom, boomdi boom,
Boomdi, boomdi, boomdi boom,
Boomdi, boomdi boom.

Pia, pia, piano, piano, piano,
Pia, pia, piano, pia, piano.

Pretend to play each instrument in turn

29

The Apple Tree

Here is the tree with leaves so green.
Here are the apples that hang between.
When the wind blows the apples fall.
Here is a basket to gather them all.

Make tree with arms

Make fists

Wave arms then let fists fall suddenly

Link hands to make a basket

HERE IS THE TREE...

HERE ARE THE APPLES...

...THE APPLES FALL

HERE IS A BASKET...

The Cherry Tree

Once I found a cherry stone,
I put it in the ground,
And when I came to look at it,
A tiny shoot I found.

The shoot grew up and up each day,
And soon became a tree.
I picked the rosy cherries then,
And ate them for my tea.

Make hole with one hand and pretend to plant stone

Slowly push finger up through 'hole'

Push hand up through hole, and hold wrist

Pretend to pick cherry from each finger and eat!

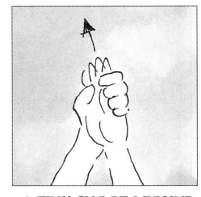
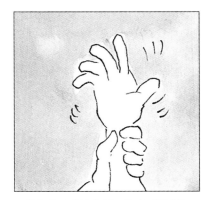
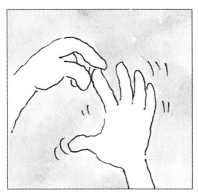

ONCE I FOUND...

...A TINY SHOOT I FOUND

...SOON BECAME A TREE

...ATE THEM FOR MY TEA

31

This is the Way the Ladies Ride

This is the way the ladies ride,
Nimble-nim, nimble-nim.

This is the way the gentlemen ride,
Gallop-a-trot, gallop-a-trot.

This is the way the farmers ride,
Hobbledy-hoy, hobbledy-hoy.

This is the way the butcher boy rides,
Tripperty-trot, tripperty-trot.

Till he falls in a ditch with a flipperty,
Flipperty, flop, flop, FLOP!

Bounce baby on knee, getting faster as rhyme progresses, and 'dropping' baby through knees on last verse

Here's a Ball for Baby

Here's a ball for baby,
Big and fat and round.

Here is baby's hammer,
See how it can pound.

Here are baby's soldiers,
Standing in a row.

Here is baby's music,
Clapping, clapping so.

Make ball with hands

BALL

Tap fist against knee

HAMMER

Show ten fingers
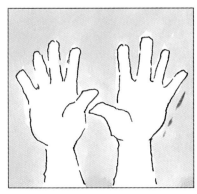
SOLDIERS

Clap hands
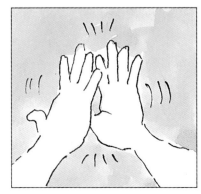
CLAPPING

Here is baby's trumpet,
TOOTLE-TOOTLE-OO!

Here's the way the baby
Plays at peek-a-boo.

Here's a big umbrella,
To keep the baby dry.

Here is baby's cradle,
Rock-a-baby-bye.

Blow through fist

TRUMPET

Hands up to eyes

PEEK-A-BOO

Pretend to hold umbrella

UMBRELLA

Rock hands in cradle

CRADLE

35

I Saw a Slippery, Slithery Snake

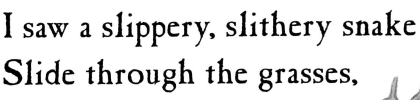

I saw a slippery, slithery snake
Slide through the grasses,
Making them shake.

Weave hands side to side

Circle eyes

He looked at me with his beady eye.

"Go away from my pretty green garden," said I.

Go away!

Repeat first action

"**Sssss**," said the slippery, slithery snake,
As he slid through the grasses,
Making them shake.

36

Foxy's Hole

Put your finger in
Foxy's hole.
Foxy's not at home.
Foxy's out at the
back door
A-picking at a bone.

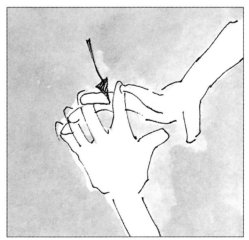

Interlock fingers leaving a hole between index and middle finger

...FINGER IN FOXY'S HOLE

Get child to put finger in hole

FOXY'S NOT AT HOME

Nip child's finger with thumbs

A-PICKING AT A BONE

The Little Bird

This little bird flaps its wings,
Flaps its wings, flaps its wings,
This little bird flaps its wings,
And flies away in the morning!

Link thumbs and flap fingers

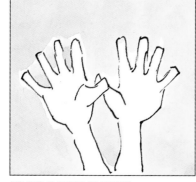

THIS LITTLE BIRD...

Lift hands ...

FLAPS ITS WINGS...

still flapping ...

FLAPS ITS WINGS...

as high as you can

FLIES AWAY...

Two Little Dicky Birds

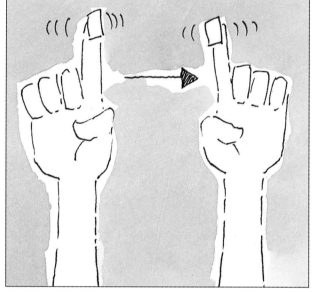

Stick paper on each index finger

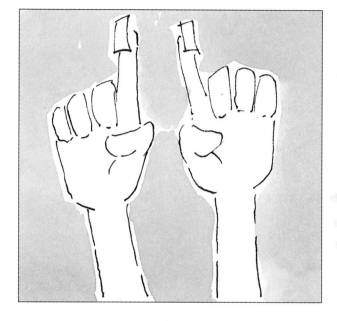

Hold out fingers and shake in turn

Two little dicky birds
Sitting on a wall,

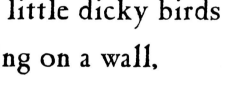

One named Peter,
One named Paul.

Toss each hand behind back

Bring back index fingers

Fly away Peter!
Fly away Paul!

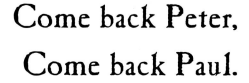

Come back Peter,
Come back Paul.

Little Cottage in the Wood

Make roof with hands

LITTLE COTTAGE

Look through hands

MAN BY THE WINDOW

Hold up fingers

RABBIT RUNNING

Knock fist in air

KNOCKING AT DOOR

Little cottage in the wood,
Little old man by the window stood,
Saw a rabbit running by,
Knocking at the door.
"Help me! Help me! Help me!" he said,
"Before the huntsman shoots me dead."
"Come little rabbit, come inside,
Safe with me abide."

Wave arms up and down

HELP ME!

Point with one finger

HUNTSMAN SHOOTS

Beckon with same finger

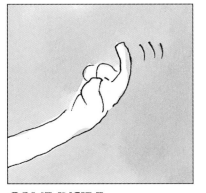

COME INSIDE

Stroke hand (rabbit)

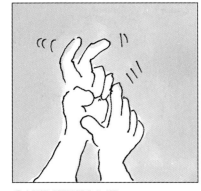

SAFE WITH ME

Gee Up, Neddy

Gee up, Neddy,
Don't you stop,
Just let your feet go
Clippety clop.
Clippety clopping,
Round and round.
Giddy up,
We're homeward bound.

Bounce baby on knee

Hickory Dickory Dock

Walk fingers up arm

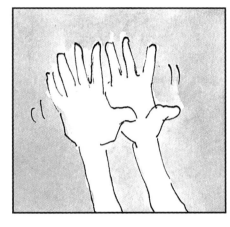

Clap once

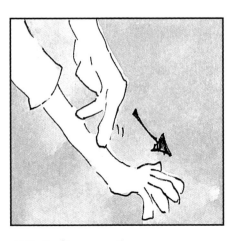

Walk fingers down arm

Hickory
dickory dock,
The mouse ran
up the clock.

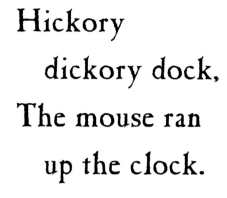

The clock
struck one,

The mouse
ran down,
Hickory
dickory dock.

There Was a Little Turtle

There was a little turtle,
He lived in a box.
He swam in a puddle,
He climbed on the rocks.

He snapped at a mosquito,
He snapped at a flea.
He snapped at a minnow,
He snapped at me.

Cup both palms, one on top of the other

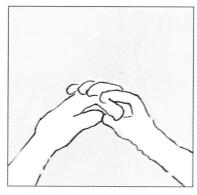

...LITTLE TURTLE

Draw a square in the air with index fingers

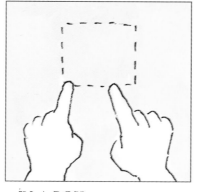

...IN A BOX

Making swimming motion with hand

...SWAM IN A PUDDLE

Waggle all five fingers in crawling motion

...ON THE ROCKS

He caught the mosquito,
He caught the flea.
He caught the minnow,

But... he didn't catch me!

Snap thumb and fingers together four times

Clap hands together three times

Shake head and point to chin

HE SNAPPED...

HE CAUGHT...

...DIDN'T CATCH ME!

Ten Little Men

Ten little men standing straight,
Ten little men open the gate,
Ten little men all in a ring,

Hold up ten fingers

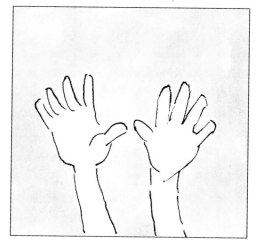

TEN LITTLE MEN...

Turn wrists

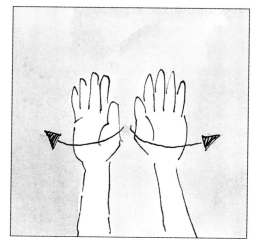

OPEN THE GATE...

Make fingers into ring

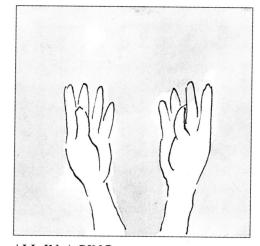

ALL IN A RING...

Ten little men bow to the king,
Ten little men dance all day,
Ten little men hide away.

Bend fingers

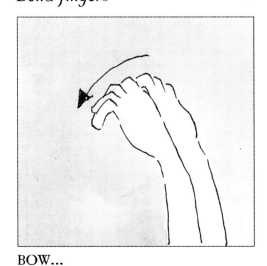

BOW...

Dance fingers

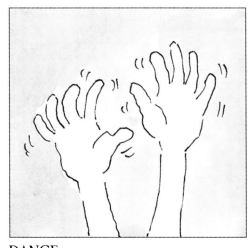

DANCE...

Hide hands behind back

HIDE AWAY

Tommy Thumb

Tommy Thumb,
Tommy Thumb,
Where are you?
Here I am, here I am,
How do you do?

Peter pointer, etc,
Middle Man, etc.
Ruby Ring, etc.
Baby Small, etc.

Make fists, raise thumbs and wiggle them

Raise forefingers and wiggle them

Raise middle fingers and wiggle them

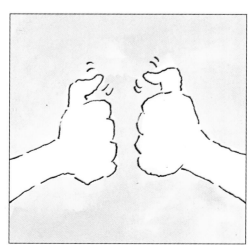

TOMMY THUMB...

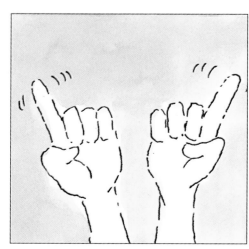

PETER POINTER...

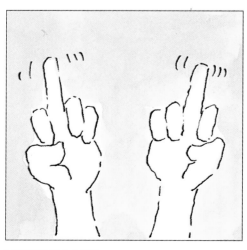

MIDDLE MAN...

48

Fingers all, fingers all,
Where are you?
Here we are, here we are,
How do you do?

Raise ring fingers and wiggle them

RUBY RING...

Raise little fingers and wiggle them

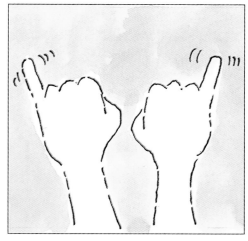

BABY SMALL...

Raise ALL fingers and wiggle them

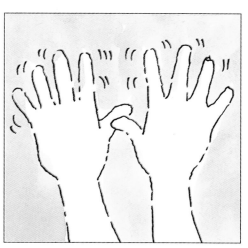

FINGERS ALL...

49

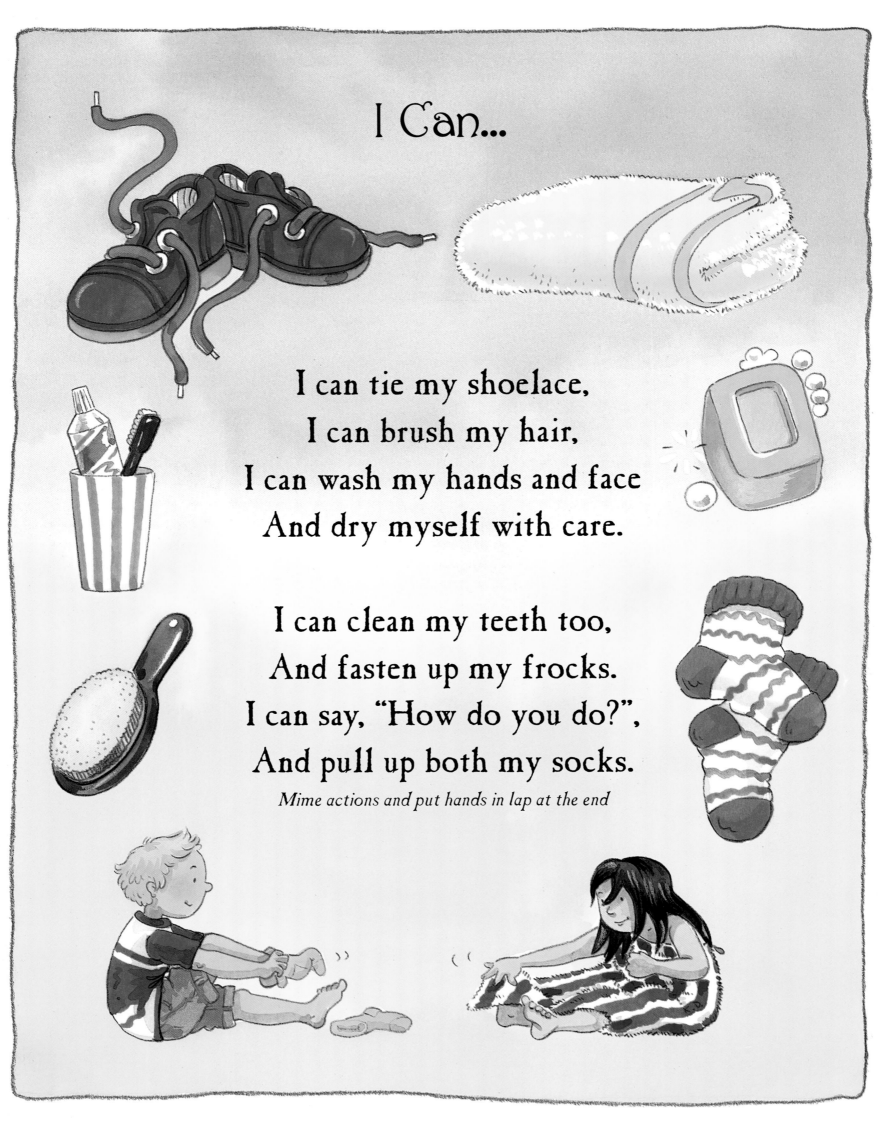

I Can...

I can tie my shoelace,
I can brush my hair,
I can wash my hands and face
And dry myself with care.

I can clean my teeth too,
And fasten up my frocks.
I can say, "How do you do?",
And pull up both my socks.

Mime actions and put hands in lap at the end

Shoes

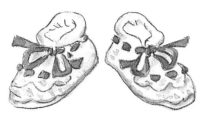

Baby's shoes,

Mother's shoes,

Father's shoes,

Policeman's shoes,

GIANT'S SHOES!

Hold hands wider apart for each pair of shoes, and make voice get louder and louder

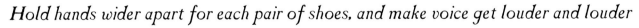

BABY'S SHOES   MOTHER'S SHOES   FATHER'S SHOES   GIANT'S SHOES!

This Little Piggy Went To Market

This little piggy went to market,

This little piggy
stayed at home,

Wiggle...

each...

toe...

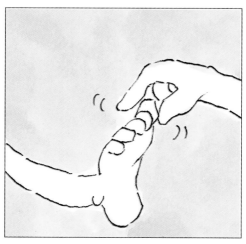

This little piggy had roast beef,

This little piggy had none,

And this little piggy cried,

"Wee-wee-wee!"

All the way home.

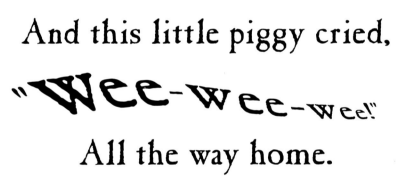

in...

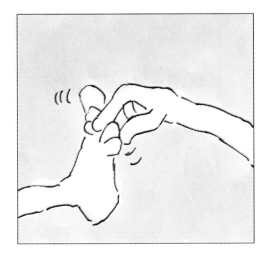

turn.

Tickle!

ALL THE WAY HOME

Peter Works with One Hammer

Peter works with one hammer,
one hammer, one hammer,
Peter works with one hammer,
this fine day.

Peter works with two hammers,
two hammers, two hammers,
Peter works with two hammers,
this fine day.

Peter works with three hammers, etc.
Peter works with four hammers, etc.
Peter works with five hammers, etc.

*Bang one fist on knee
in rhythm*

ONE HAMMER

Bang two fists on knees

TWO HAMMERS

*Bang two fists, tap
one foot*

THREE HAMMERS

*Bang two fists, tap
two feet*

FOUR HAMMERS

Peter's very tired now,
tired now, tired now,
Peter's very tired now,
this fine day.

Peter's going to sleep now,
sleep now, sleep now,
Peter's going to sleep now,
this fine day.

Peter's waking up now,
up now, up now,
Peter's waking up now,
this fine day.

*Bang two fists, tap two
feet and nod head*

FIVE HAMMERS

*Rub eyes and stretch
as if yawning*

TIRED NOW

Pretend to sleep

GOING TO SLEEP

*Pretend to wake
and stretch*

WAKING UP

Sing-Along Songs

A collection of traditional
sing-along songs to
enjoy together.

Dance To Your Daddy

Dance to your daddy,
My little babby;
Dance to your daddy,
My little lamb.
You shall have a fishy
On a little dishy,
You shall have a fishy
When the boat comes in.

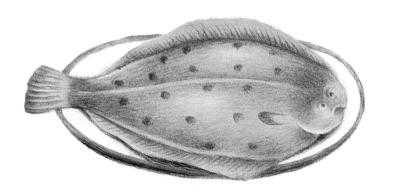

Humpty Dumpty

Humpty Dumpty sat on a wall;
Humpty Dumpty had a great fall;
All the King's horses, and all the King's men
Couldn't put Humpty together again.

Knick Knack Paddy Whack

This old man, he played one,

He played knick knack on my drum.

With a knick knack paddy whack, give a dog a bone,

This old man went rolling home.

This old man, he played two,

He played knick knack on my shoe.

With a knick knack paddy whack, give a dog a bone,

This old man went rolling home.

This old man, he played three,
He played knick knack on my knee.
With a knick knack paddy whack, give a dog a bone,
This old man went rolling home.

This old man, he played four,
He played knick knack on my door.
With a knick knack paddy whack, give a dog a bone,
This old man went rolling home.

This old man, he played five,
He played knick knack on my hive.
With a knick knack paddy whack, give a dog a bone,
This old man went rolling home.

Little Boy Blue

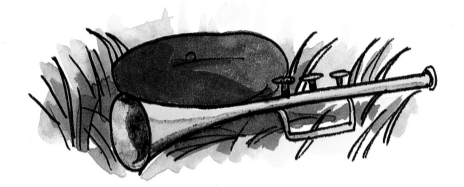

Little Boy Blue, come blow your horn

The sheep's in the meadow, the cow's in the corn.

Where is the boy who looks after the sheep?

He's under the haystack fast asleep.

Will you wake him? No, not I!

For if I do, he's sure to cry.

Yankee Doodle

Yankee Doodle came to town,
Riding on a pony,
He stuck a feather in his cap
And called it macaroni.

The Man In The Moon

The man in the moon
Came down too soon,
And asked his way to Norwich;
He went by the south,
And burnt his mouth
By eating cold plum porridge.

NORWICH

Rock-a-Bye-Baby

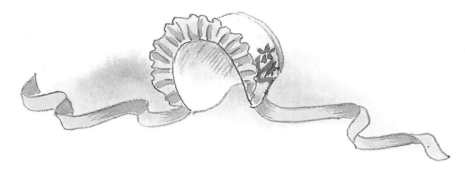

Rock-a-bye baby, on the tree top;

When the wind blows, the cradle will rock;

When the bough breaks, the cradle will fall;

Down will come baby, cradle and all.

Pease Pudding Hot

Pease pudding hot,
Pease pudding cold,
Pease pudding in the pot,
Nine days old.

Some like it hot,
Some like it cold,
Some like it in the pot,
Nine days old.

Sing a Song of Sixpence

Sing a song of sixpence,

A pocket full of rye;

Four-and-twenty blackbirds baked in a pie;

When the pie was opened,

The birds began to sing;

Wasn't that a dainty dish,

To set before a king?

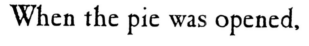
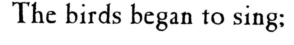

It's Raining, It's Pouring

It's raining, it's pouring,
The old man is snoring.
He went to bed,
And bumped his head,
And couldn't get up
in the morning.

Lavender's Blue

Lavender's blue, dilly, dilly, lavender's green,
When I am king, dilly, dilly, you shall be queen;
Call up your men, dilly dilly, set them to work,
Some to the plough, dilly dilly, some to the cart;
Some to make hay, dilly, dilly, some to thresh corn;
Whilst you and I, dilly, dilly, keep ourselves warm.

The Farmer's in his Den

The farmer's in his den,

The farmer's in his den,

E I E I

The farmer's in his den.

The farmer wants a wife,

The farmer wants a wife,

E I E I

The farmer wants a wife.

The wife wants a child,

The wife wants a child,

E I E I

The wife wants a child.

The child wants a nurse,
The child wants a nurse,
E I E I
The child wants a nurse.

The nurse wants a dog,
The nurse wants a dog,
E I E I
The nurse wants a dog.

We all pat the dog,
We all pat the dog,
E I E I
We all pat the dog.

Goosey Goosey Gander

Goosey, goosey, gander,

Whither shall I wander?

Upstairs and downstairs,

And in my lady's chamber.

There I met an old man

Who would not say his prayers.

I took him by the left leg

And threw him down the stairs.

London Bridge is Falling Down

London bridge is falling down,
Falling down, falling down,
London bridge is falling down,
My fair lady.

Build it up with wood and clay,
Wood and clay, wood and clay,
Build it up with wood and clay,
My fair lady.

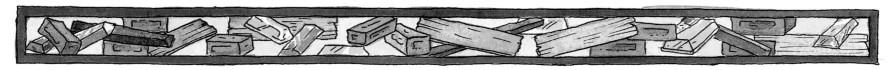

Wood and clay will wash away,
Wash away, wash away,
Wood and clay will wash away,
My fair lady.

Build it up with bricks and mortar,
Bricks and mortar, bricks and mortar,
Build it up with bricks and mortar,
My fair lady.

Bricks and mortar will not stay,
Will not stay, will not stay,
Bricks and mortar will not stay,
My fair lady.

Build it up with iron and steel,
Iron and steel, iron and steel,
Build it up with iron and steel,
My fair lady.

Iron and steel will bend and bow,
Bend and bow, bend and bow
Iron and steel will bend and bow,
My fair lady.

Build it up with silver and gold,
Silver and gold, silver and gold,
Build it up with silver and gold,
My fair lady.

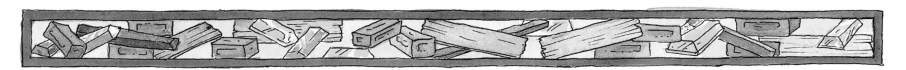

Silver and gold will be stolen away,
Stolen away, stolen away,
Silver and gold will be stolen away,
My fair lady.

Set a man to watch all night,
Watch all night, watch all night,
Set a man to watch all night,
My fair lady.

Simple Simon

Simple Simon met a pieman
Going to the fair,
Says Simple Simon to the pieman
"Let me taste your ware."
Says the pieman to Simple Simon,
"Show me first your penny."
Says Simple Simon to the pieman,
"Indeed I have not any."

Simple Simon went a-fishing
For to catch a whale;
But all the water he had got
Was in his mother's pail.

One Man Went To Mow

One man went to mow, went to mow a meadow,
One man and his dog, Spot,
Went to mow a meadow.

Two men went to mow, went to mow a meadow,
Two men, one man and his dog, Spot,
Went to mow a meadow.

Three men went to mow, went to mow a meadow,

Three men, two men, one man and his dog, Spot,

Went to mow a meadow.

Four men went to mow, went to mow a meadow,

Four men, three men, two men, one man and his dog, Spot,

Went to mow a meadow.

Five men went to mow, went to mow a meadow,

Five men, four men, three men, two men,

one man and his dog, Spot,

Went to mow a meadow.

Old MacDonald

Old MacDonald had a farm,

E...I...E...I...O

And on that farm he had some cows,

E...I...E...I...O

With a moo-moo here,

And a moo-moo there,

Here a moo, there a moo,

Everywhere a moo-moo,

Old MacDonald had a farm,

E...I...E...I...O

Old MacDonald had a farm,

E...I...E...I...O

And on that farm he had some ducks,

E...I...E...I...O

With a quack-quack here,

And a quack-quack there, *etc.*

This rhyme can be continued with other verses: sheep, baa-baa; dogs, woof-woof; horses, neigh-neigh; cats, miaow-miaow; etc. The speed can be adjusted to suit the age of the child. Older children can memorise the previous verses and add them to the rhyme, eg. 'with a quack-quack here, and a quack-quack there, here a quack, there a quack, everywhere a quack, quack, moo-moo here, moo-moo there,' etc.

Pussy Cat, Pussy Cat

Pussy cat, pussy cat, where have you been?

I've been up to London to visit the Queen.

Pussy cat, pussy cat, what did you there?

I frightened a little mouse under her chair.

Diddle, Diddle, Dumpling

Diddle, diddle, dumpling, my son John,

Went to bed with his trousers on;

One shoe off, one shoe on,

Diddle, diddle, dumpling, my son John.

There Was a Crooked Man

There was a crooked man
And he walked a crooked mile,
He found a crooked sixpence
Against a crooked stile.
He brought a crooked cat
Which caught a crooked mouse
And they all lived together
In a little crooked house.

A Frog He Would A-Wooing Go

A frog he would a-wooing go,

Heigh ho! says Rowley,

Whether his mother would let him or no,

With a rowley, powley, gammon and spinach,

Heigh ho! says Anthony Rowley.

So off he set with his opera hat,

Heigh ho! says Rowley,

And on the way he met with a rat,

With a rowley, powley, gammon and spinach,

Heigh ho! says Anthony Rowley.

Lazy Mary

Lazy Mary will you get up,

Will you get up, will you get up?

Lazy Mary will you get up,

Will you get up today?

Six o'clock and you're still sleeping,

Daylight's creeping o'er your windowsill.

Lazy Mary will you get up,

Will you get up, will you get up?

Lazy Mary will you get up,

Will you get up today?

Seven o'clock and you're still snoring,
Sunshine's pouring through your window pane.

Lazy Mary will you get up,
Will you get up, will you get up?
Lazy Mary will you get up,
Will you get up today?

Eight o'clock, you've missed your train,
Can you explain why you're still in your bed?

Old Mother Hubbard

Old Mother Hubbard
Went to the cupboard
To fetch her poor dog a bone,
But when she got there
The cupboard was bare
And so the poor dog had none.

Ten Green Bottles

Ten green bottles, standing on a wall,

Ten green bottles, standing on a wall,

And if one green bottle should accidentally fall,

There'd be nine green bottles, standing on a wall.

(continue with nine green bottles etc...)

Grand Old Duke of York

The grand old Duke of York,

He had ten thousand men;

He marched them up to the top of the hill;

Then he marched them down again.

And when they were up they were up.

And when they were down they were down.

And when they were only halfway up,

They were neither up nor down.

Tom, Tom The Piper's Son

Tom, Tom, the piper's son,

Stole a pig and away he run!

The pig was eat, and Tom was beat,

And Tom went roaring down the street.

Mary, Mary, Quite Contrary

Mary, Mary, quite contrary,
How does your garden grow?
With silver bells and cockle shells
And pretty maids all in a row.

A Tisket, A Tasket

A tisket, a tasket,
A green and yellow basket.
I wrote a letter to my love,
And on the way I dropped it.

I dropped it, I dropped it,
And on the way I dropped it.
A little girl picked it up
And put it in her pocket.

Ding Dong Bell

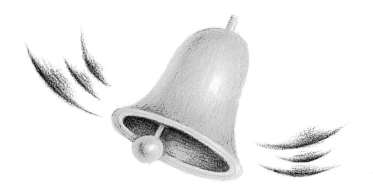

Ding, dong, bell,

Pussy's in the well!

Who put her in?

Little Tommy Green.

Who pulled her out?

Little Johnny Stout.

What a naughty boy was that

To try to drown poor pussy cat,

Who never did any harm,

But killed the mice in his father's barn.

The Muffin Man

Have you seen the muffin man,
The muffin man, the muffin man?
Have you seen the muffin man,
He lives in Drury Lane?
Oh yes, I've seen the muffin man,
The muffin man, the muffin man.
Oh yes, I've seen the muffin man,
He lives in Drury Lane.

Old King Cole

Old King Cole was a merry old soul,
And a merry old soul was he;
He called for his pipe,
And he called for his bowl,
And he called for his fiddlers three.

Animal Tales

Written by Caroline Repchuk

Entertaining animal tales and rhymes for you to enjoy.

WHALE SONG

"Oh, what a beautiful morning!" sang Flippy, the whale, as streaks of sunlight filtered down through the clear blue ocean. He swam to and fro, twirled around, then whooshed up through the waves, and jumped clear of the water in a perfect pirouette.

Flippy loved to sing and dance. The trouble was, although he was a very graceful dancer, his singing was terrible. His big mouth would open wide, as he boomed out song after song — but none of them were in tune! The dreadful sound echoed through the ocean for miles, sending all the fish and other ocean creatures diving into the rocks and reefs for cover, as the waters shook around them. It was always worse when the sun shone, as the bright warm sun made Flippy want to sing and dance with happiness. It had got so bad that the other creatures had begun to pray for dull skies and rain.

"Something has got to be done!" complained Wobble, the jellyfish. "Flippy's booming voice makes me quiver and shake so much that I can't see where I'm going!"

"Well, I know where I'm going," said Snappy, the lobster. "As far away as possible. My head is splitting from Flippy's awful wailing."

"Someone will have to tell Flippy not to sing anymore," said Sparky, the stingray.

"But it will hurt his feelings," said Wobble.

"Not as much as his singing hurts my ears!" snapped Snappy.

And so they decided that Sparky would tell Flippy the next day that they did not want him to sing any more songs. Wobble was right. Flippy was very upset when he heard that the others did not like his singing. He cried big, salty tears.

"I was only trying to enjoy myself!" he sobbed. "I didn't realise I was upsetting everyone else."

"There, there," said Sparky, wishing he had not been chosen to give the little whale the bad news. "You can still enjoy dancing."

"It's not the same without music," said Flippy, miserably. "You can't get the rhythm." And he swam off into the deep waters, saying he wanted to be alone for a while.

As Flippy lay on the bottom of the ocean floor, feeling very sorry for himself, a beautiful sound came floating through the water from far away in the distance. It sounded like someone singing. Flippy wanted to know who was making such a lovely sound, so with a flick of his big tail, he set off in the direction it was coming from.

As he got closer, he could hear a soft voice singing a beautiful melody. Peering out from behind a big rock, he saw that the voice belonged to a little octopus, who was shuffling and swaying about on the ocean floor. His legs seemed to be going in all directions, as he stumbled and tripped along.

Then he tried to spin around, but his legs got tangled and he crashed to the ground in a heap.

"Oh, dear," said Leggy, the octopus. "I seem to have eight left feet!"

Flippy looked out shyly from behind the rock.

"What are you trying to do?" he asked.

The little octopus looked rather embarrassed.

"I was trying to dance," he said, blushing pink.

"Only I'm not very good at it."

"Well, maybe I could teach you," said Flippy. "I'm a very good dancer. And in return, there is something that I would love you to teach me!"

A few weeks later, Wobble, Snappy and Sparky were discussing how they missed having Flippy around, when they heard a strange and beautiful sound floating towards them through the ocean.

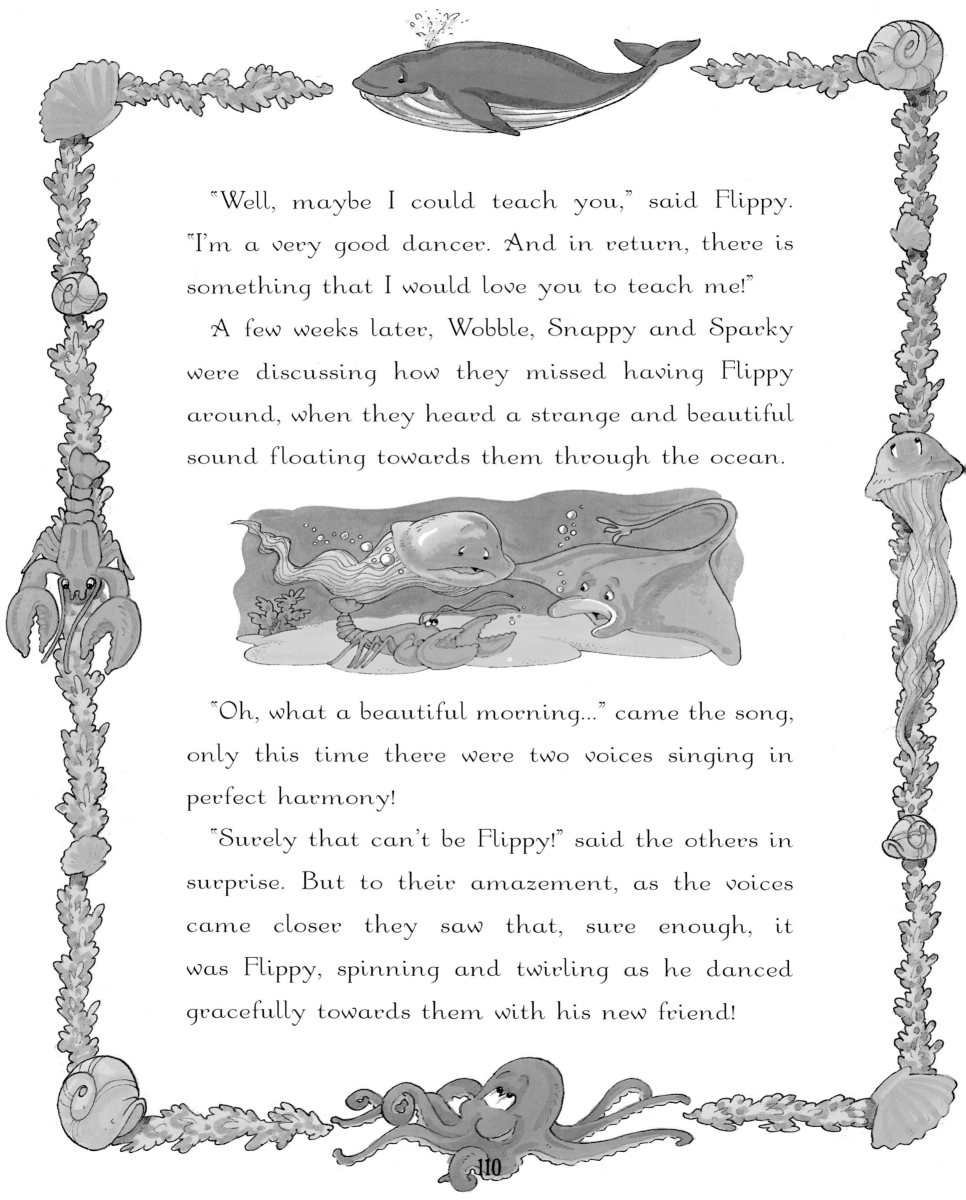

"Oh, what a beautiful morning..." came the song, only this time there were two voices singing in perfect harmony!

"Surely that can't be Flippy!" said the others in surprise. But to their amazement, as the voices came closer they saw that, sure enough, it was Flippy, spinning and twirling as he danced gracefully towards them with his new friend!

LITTLE SHEEP

Little Sheep couldn't sleep,
Not a wink, not a peep!
Tossing, turning, all night through,
What was poor Little Sheep to do?

Owl came by, old and wise,
Said, "Silly sheep, use your eyes –
You're lying in a field of sheep,
Try counting them to help you sleep!"

"Seven, four, thirteen, ten –
That's not right, I'll start again..."
Till daylight came, awake he lay
And vowed he'd learn to count next day!

GIRAFFE'S SONG

It's wonderful having a long neck,
That reaches right up to the sky,
You can nibble the leaves on the treetops,
And smile at the birds flying by.

It's wonderful having a long neck,
You can see for miles around,
You always know just where
your friends are,
And where the best food can be found.

It's wonderful having a long neck,
Although, I'm not meaning to gloat.
For there's one time that I really curse it,
And that's when I get a sore throat!

CROCODILE SMILES

"Say cheese!" said the photographer.

"CHEESE!" grinned Snappy, the crocodile. Lights flashed, and cameras clicked as he gave his most winning smile.

"You're a natural!" cried the expedition leader. He was with a team of wildlife photographers. Snappy smiled at his reflection in the river.

"Ooh, you are a handsome chap!" he preened, gnashing his fine set of teeth together with glee.

Snappy was terribly proud of his sharp fangs, and fine good looks. He strutted up and down the river bank for all to see.

"I'm a star!" he said. "My face will be known throughout the world!"

"Thanks for letting us take your picture," said the expedition leader.

"No problem," said Snappy. "Anytime!"

"And as your reward, here's the truckload of chocolate you asked for," said the leader.

"How delicious!" said Snappy. "Most kind of you. Thank you so much."

When they had gone, Snappy lay sunning himself on the river bank, daydreaming of fame and fortune, and popping chocolate after chocolate into his big, open mouth.

Just then, along slithered Snake.

"What's thissss?" he hissed. "A crocodile eating chocolate? How sssstrange!"

"Not at all!" snapped Snappy. "All crocodiles love chocolate. It's just that most of them aren't clever enough to know how to get hold of it."

"Well, if you're so sssmart, you ssshould know that too much chocolate will make your teeth fall out!" hissed Snake.

"What rot!" said Snappy, crossly. "For your information, I've got perfect teeth."

"Lucky you!" said Snake, and slithered off into the bushes.

So Snappy carried on munching happily, eating his way through the mound of chocolate. He had chocolate for breakfast, chocolate for lunch and chocolate for dinner.

"Ooh, yummy!" he grinned, licking his lips and smiling a big, chocolatey smile. "This is heaven."

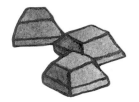

"You won't be saying that when you are too fat to float in the river," said Parrot, who had been watching him from a tree.

"Nonsense!" scoffed Snappy. "I've got a very fine figure, I'll have you know!"

"If you say so," said Parrot, and flew off into the jungle.

Days and weeks passed, and Snappy happily carried on eating chocolate after chocolate, until at last it was all gone.

"Back to the river to catch my next meal, then," Snappy thought miserably. "Though I'd much rather have more chocolate!"

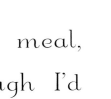

But when Snappy slid into the river, instead of bobbing gently at the surface, he sank straight to the bottom, and his stomach rested in the mud.

"Oh, dear, what's happened to the river?" Snappy wondered aloud to himself. "It's very hard to float in today."

"Even for someone with such a fine figure as you?" jeered Parrot, watching from the trees. Snappy didn't answer. He just sank further beneath the water so that only his two beady eyes could be seen, and gave Parrot a very hard stare.

The next morning when he awoke there was a terrible pain in his mouth. It felt like someone was twisting and tugging on his teeth. "Oww, my teeth hurt!" he cried.

"Sssurely not!" hissed Snake, dangling down from a tree. "After all, you have sssuch perfect teeth!" and he slunk away again, snickering.

Snappy knew what he had to do. He set off down the river to visit Mr Drill the dentist.

It seemed such a long hard walk, and by the time he got there he was puffing and panting.

"Open wide!" said Mr Drill, an anteater, peering down his long nose into Snappy's gaping mouth. "Oh, dear. This doesn't look good at all. What have you been eating, Snappy? Now show me where it hurts."

"Here," said Snappy pointing miserably into his mouth, and feeling rather ashamed, "and here, and here, and here..."

"Well, there's nothing for it," said Mr Drill, "they'll have to come out!" And so out they came!

Before long, another photography expedition arrived in the jungle.

"Say cheese!" said the expedition leader.

"CHEESE!" smiled Snappy, stepping out from behind a tree. But instead of a flash of cameras, Snappy met with howls of laughter, as the photographers fell about holding their sides.

"I thought you said Snappy was a handsome crocodile with perfect teeth!" they cried, looking at the leader. "He should be called Gappy, not Snappy!"

Poor Snappy slunk away into the bushes and cried. It was all his own fault for being so greedy and eating all that chocolate.

"There, there," said Mr Drill, patting his arm. "We'll soon fit you out with some fine new teeth."

And from then on, Snappy vowed he would never eat chocolate again!

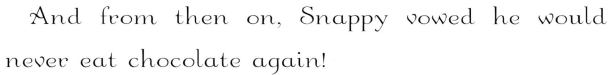

ELEPHANTS NEVER FORGET

I woke up this morning, astounded,
To find my long trunk in a knot!
I know it must be to remind me
To remember something I've forgot!

But though I've been thinking all morning
I haven't remembered it yet.
Still I'm sure I will think of it soon,
Because elephants never forget!

ITCHY SPOTS

Poor Monkey was wriggling
And jiggling around,
Scratching and making
A chattering sound:

"They're driving me mad,
Someone help me please –
I have to get rid of
These terrible fleas!"

Then along came a bear
In a bit of a stew –
"I've got such a bad itch,
I don't know what to do!

It's right in a spot
I can't reach with my paws.
So why not scratch my back,
And I will scratch yours!"

LEAP FROG

"Whee! Look at me! Look at me!" yelled Springy, the frog, as he went leaping through the air, jumping from one lily pad to the other with a great splash. "I'm the bounciest frog in the whole wide world! Whee!"

"Tut, tut!" quacked Mother Duck. "That young frog is a nuisance. He never looks where he's going, and he doesn't mind who he splashes."

"Quite dreadful," agreed Downy, the swan. "And he makes so much noise. Sometimes it's hard to hear yourself think!"

But Springy wasn't listening. He was far too busy jumping across the lily pads as high as he could.

"Come on!" he called to the little ducklings. "Come over here, we'll have a diving contest!"

The ducklings shook their tails with excitement as they hurried across the pond towards him, then splashed about ducking and diving.

"He's a bad influence on our youngsters," Mother Duck went on. "If only something could be done about him."

"I suppose it's just high spirits," said Downy. "He'll grow out of it."

But Springy didn't grow out of it — he grew worse. He would wake everyone up at the crack of dawn, singing loudly at the top of his croaky voice:

"Here comes the day, it's time to play, hip hooray, hip hooray!" And he would leap from place to place, waking up the ducks and swans in their nests, calling down Rabbit's burrow, and shouting into Water Rat's hole in the bank. Of course, Springy just thought that he was being friendly. He didn't realize that everyone was getting fed up with him.

"I'm all for a bit of fun," said Water Rat. "But young Springy always takes things too far."

Then one day, Springy appeared almost bursting with excitement.

"Listen everyone," he called. "There's going to be a jumping competition on the other side of the pond. All the other frogs from miles around are coming. But I'm sure to win, because I'm the bounciest frog in the whole wide world!" And with that he jumped high up in the air, just to prove it was true.

The day of the contest dawned, and everyone gathered at the far side of the pond to watch the competition. Springy had never seen so many frogs in one place before.

"Wait till they see how high I can jump!" he said, leaping up and down in excitement.

But to Springy's amazement, all the frogs could jump high, and far too. They sprang gracefully across the lily pads, cheered on by the crowd.

Springy was going to have to jump higher and further than ever if he wanted to win. At last it was his turn. "Good luck!" cried the ducklings.

Springy took his place on the starting pad, then gathering all his strength, he leapt up high and flew through the air, further and further, past the finish line, and on, until – GULP! He landed right in crafty Pike's waiting open mouth! As usual, Springy had not been looking where he was going!

The naughty pike swallowed Springy in one gulp, then dived down and hid in the middle of the pond. Everyone looked around in dismay — there was nothing they could do. Springy was gone.

Well, there was no doubt about it. Springy had jumped the highest, and the furthest.

"I declare Springy the winner," Warty, the toad, who had organised the contest, said glumly. So everyone went home, feeling sad and empty.

After that, things were much quieter for the other folk that lived around the pond.

But instead of enjoying the peace, they found that they rather missed Springy.

"He was a cheery little frog," said Downy.

"My young ones miss him terribly," said Mother Duck. "I suppose he did keep them busy."

But deep in the pond, Pike was feeling sorry for himself. He thought he'd been very clever catching that frog, but he'd had terrible indigestion ever since. You see, Springy was still busy jumping away inside him! Pike rose up to the top of the water, and gulped at the air. And as he did so, out jumped Springy!

Everyone was delighted to see him, and cheered as they gave him the medal for winning the jumping contest.

"This is wonderful," said Springy. "But I have learned my lesson — from now on I'll look before I leap!" and he hopped away quietly to play with the ducklings.

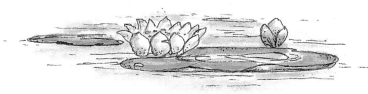

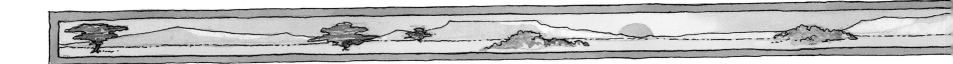

LAZY LION

Lazy Lion lay snoozing in the shade of a tree. The hot sun beat down, as he lazily flicked at the buzzing flies with his tail.

There was nothing Lazy Lion liked to do more than sleep. He would sleep all night and all day if he could, just waking up every once in a while to have a snack.

"Hmm," he purred to himself. "This is the life. Nothing to do all day but lie in the sun and sleep. Perfect!"

Just then, a laughing hyena came running by.

"Wake up, Lazy Lion!" he chuckled. "Unless you feel like going for a swim!? Rain's coming!"

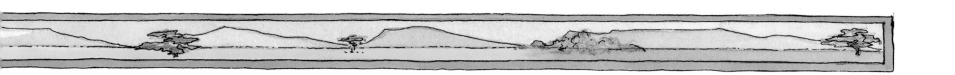

Lazy Lion opened one eye. "Silly creature!" he said with a sniff, as he watched the hyena running far off into the distance, still laughing. "He's just trying to trick me into waking up and moving!" and he closed his eyes and went back to sleep.

A short while later someone nudged his behind. "Wake up, Lazy Lion. Rain's coming." Giraffe was bending her long neck down and nudging him with her nose. "You should head for shelter. The river might flood!"

"Don't be ridiculous!" said Lion. "Hyena's been filling your head with his nonsense, I see!" and he closed his eyes and was snoring again in seconds.

But he had not been dozing for long when he felt something tugging at his whiskers.

"Wake up, Lazy Lion!" It was a little mouse.

"Rain's coming. Could you please carry my children and I to safety?" asked the mouse.

"Oh, I'm far too busy for that," said Lazy Lion. "Besides, what's all this talk of rain? It's a fine, sunny day!" And with that, he closed his eyes and went back to sleep.

A few moments later he was woken by something pulling at his tail. It was Monkey.

"Wake up, Lazy Lion. Rain's coming. Could you help carry my bananas up to the rocks?"

"Why does everyone keep waking me?" asked Lazy Lion, crossly. "Can't you see I'm busy?"

"Sorry, Lion, but you didn't look busy to me," said Monkey.

"Well, I am!" growled Lion. "I'm very busy thinking what to do with the next person who wakes me up!" And he gave Monkey a mean stare, before shutting his eyes tight once more.

After that, none of the animals dared to wake Lazy Lion up again. So they couldn't warn him that the dark storm clouds were gathering, and the first drops of rain had started to fall.

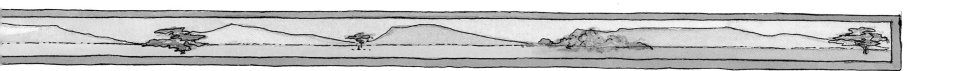

They just hurried high up to the safety of the rocks and caves and took shelter from the storm that was on its way.

Lazy Lion gave a little shiver, as he lay dreaming. A big raindrop fell on his nose. Then another, and another. Lion stirred. "Oh, bother," he thought to himself. "It's raining. Well, it's probably only a light shower. I'll snooze a little longer." He settled back down to sleep.

But the rain began to fall harder, and harder. Soon Lazy Lion's thick fur was wet through, and he was starting to feel cold and uncomfortable. But he was still too lazy to get up and move to the shelter of the rocks. "I'll just sleep for five more minutes!" he told himself.

But as the minutes passed the rain fell harder and harder, and the river rose higher and higher. Then, with a huge crash of thunder, and a bright flash of lightening, the river broke its banks and came flooding across the plains! All of a sudden, Lazy Lion found himself being tossed around as he struggled to keep his head above the stormy waters.

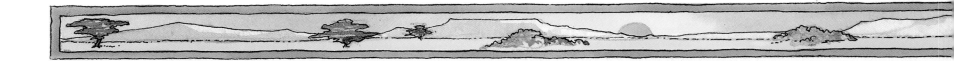

The other animals watched in horror from the safety of the rocks as Lazy Lion was dragged below the water by the strong current.

Then suddenly his big strong head popped up again, and he gasped for breath.

Lazy Lion swam with all his might towards the rocks, as the other animals cheered him on.

"Oh, this is hard work!" he panted. How he wished he had listened to the others and had not been so lazy.

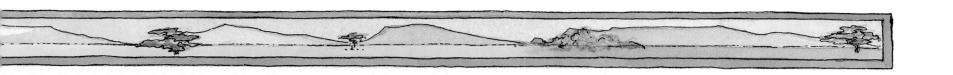

At last he made it, and he struggled up onto the rocks, wet through and worn out. The other animals gathered round, anxiously.

"Are you all right, Lazy Lion?" asked Monkey.

"I'm exhausted!" panted Lazy Lion, then added, "But it's nothing a good sleep won't cure!"

MESSAGE IN A BOTTLE

Frosty, the polar bear, dipped a huge hairy paw into a hole in the ice and felt about. He was sure he had seen something glimmering beneath the surface of the water. Just then, Beaky, the penguin, popped up through the hole, clutching something under his wing. It was a glass bottle.

"I thought I saw something odd," said Frosty. "What is it?"

"I don't know," said Beaky. "I found it in the sea, far away on the other side of the icebergs. It was floating on the waves."

The two friends sat and looked at the bottle.

"There's something inside," said Beaky. "Let's take it out." They took out the cork and Beaky reached inside with his beak and pulled out a note.

"What does it say?" asked Frosty.

Beaky peered closely at the note.

"It says: 'Help. I am stranded on a desert island. My boat is broken. It is very hot. Love Browny, the bear,'" read Beaky. "There's a map on the other side. Do you think we should help?"

"Of course we should," said Frosty. "It sounds like one of my cousins is in trouble. Anyway, it will be a great adventure! I've always wanted to know what hot feels like!"

The two friends studied the map carefully, then set off across the ice and snow until they reached the sea. They turned and waved goodbye to their chilly home, dived into the icy water and started to swim south in the direction of the desert island. After a while, Frosty began to feel tired. He had never swum so far away from home before.

"Let's rest a moment," said Beaky, and they flipped over in the water and lay floating along on their backs.

"Do you think it's much further?" asked Frosty.

"Oh, yes, much further," said Beaky. "The water has not even begun to get warm yet. By the time we get there it will be like taking a hot bath."

"I've never had one of those!" said Frosty, excitedly. "Will I like it?"

"I'm not sure," said Beaky.

So the two friends carried on swimming towards the sunshine. Gradually the water grew warmer and warmer. Frosty started to laugh.

"My skin's all nice and tingly," he chuckled.

On and on they swam. The bright sun beat down on their heads. By now Frosty was puffing and panting with every stroke.

"I think I must be feeling hot," he said. "I don't think I can swim much further!

"You don't have to!" said Beaky, pointing with his wing. "There's the island!"

On the shore, Browny was jumping up and down with excitement and waving his paws.

"You found me!" he cried. "Imagine my little bottle floating all the way to the North Pole!"

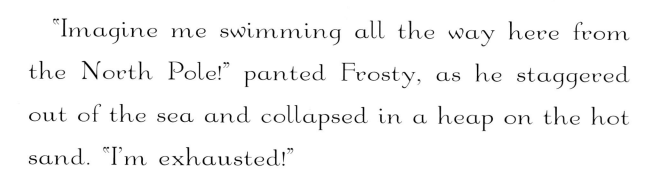

"Imagine me swimming all the way here from the North Pole!" panted Frosty, as he staggered out of the sea and collapsed in a heap on the hot sand. "I'm exhausted!"

Browny led his rescuers to the shelter of a cave he had found nearby, and they rested there until they recovered. As night fell, Browny built a fire on the beach, and they sat telling stories. He told them all about finding a little boat and setting sail across the sea, and how his boat had been shipwrecked.

"I thought I would be stranded here for ever!" Browny said. "And I want to go home!"

"Don't worry," said Frosty. "We'll get you home. But first let's get a good night's rest."

The next morning the three friends had great fun playing on the beach.

"I'm not sure I like hot, though," said Frosty, "it makes me tired and uncomfortable. And this sand stuff gets everywhere!" The others laughed.

"Let's be on our way then," said Beaky.

And so they set back off across the ocean, pulling Browny along on a raft he'd made, as he wasn't a good swimmer like the others. It was another long, hard journey, but when they finally reached Browny's home and saw how happy he was to be back there, they knew it was worth it.

"Promise you'll come and visit me again!" cried Browny, as the others waved goodbye and set off once more for their chilly home.

"We will!" cried Frosty. "But not if you're somewhere hot. I can't wait to get home for a good slide on the ice!"

Teddy Tales

Written by Caroline Repchuk, Claire Keen and Andrew Charman

A teddy tale for everyone, and some teddy rhymes too!

THE NAUGHTY BEARS

One sunny summer's day, Ben and Fraser's parents told them to pack their things, as they were going to the beach.

"Yippee!" said Ben. "Can we take our teddies?"

"As long as you keep an eye on them," said Daddy. "We don't want to spend all afternoon looking for them if you lose them again!"

Ben and Fraser took their teddies everywhere they went, but they were always losing them, and then there was a great hunt to find them. But the truth was, that when no one was looking, the naughty little teddies would run away in search of excitement and adventure.

Today was no different. The family arrived at the beach and unpacked their things. Daddy sat reading a newspaper and Mommy took out a book. Soon Ben and Fraser were busy building sandcastles. When the naughty teddies saw that no one was looking, they jumped up and ran away giggling, all along the beach.

"Let's go exploring," said Billy, who was the oldest bear. "I can see a cave over there." He pointed to a dark hole in the rocks close to the water.

"It looks a bit dark and scary," said Bella.

"Don't be silly," said Billy. "You're a bear. Bears like dark caves!"

The little bears clambered over the rocks and into the cave. It was very deep, and very dark. Just then, Bella spotted something gleaming on the floor. She picked it up and showed it to Billy.

"Gold!" said Billy, in excitement, taking the little coin from Bella. "This must be a smuggler's cave! Maybe the smugglers are still here. Let's take a look!"

"No!" said Bella. "They could be dangerous. Let's go back." She turned and ran back outside, where she saw to her horror that while they had been exploring the tide had come in, and cut the rocks off from the beach.

"Billy!" she called. "Come quick, we're stranded!"

Meanwhile, Ben and Fraser had finished making sandcastles and found that their teddy bears were missing.

"Oh, no," groaned Daddy. "Not again!"

The family hunted high and low along the beach, but there was no sign of the bears to be found. "Maybe they've been washed out to sea," said Fraser, his voice trembling at the thought.

Back at the cave the naughty teddies could see their owners looking for them. They jumped up and down and waved their paws. "It's no use," said Bella, "they can't see us. We're too small."

"Don't worry," said Billy, trying to sound braver than he felt.

Just then, two men appeared from the other side of the rocks. The teddies froze – these must be the smugglers! They trembled in fear as the men picked them up, clambered over the rocks, and tossed them into a little boat that had been hidden from view. The teddies clung together at the bottom of the boat as the men jumped in and began to row. Where were they taking them?

After a while, the boat stopped and one of the
men jumped out. He grabbed the bears and held
them in the air high above his head, calling out,
"Has anyone lost these bears?"

Everyone on the beach looked up, and Ben and
Fraser raced over and grabbed their bears.

"Thank you," said Daddy. "We've been looking
everywhere for them."

"We found them up by that cave," said one of
the men, pointing over to the cave. "Your kids
must have left them there."

"But they've been here building sandcastles all afternoon..." said Daddy, looking puzzled.

No one ever did find out how the naughty teddies got to the cave, or where the little coin in Billy's pocket came from. But from then on Daddy said they had to stay at home. The naughty teddies didn't really mind. They'd had enough adventures for the time being. And it gave them lots of time to play their favorite game – hide and seek!

MY BEST FRIEND

He cuddles me at bedtime,
And keeps me safe at night,
If I have a bad dream,
And wake up in a fright.

He is my constant playmate,
And often shares my tea,
He always lets me win at games,
And has a smile for me.

He shares in all my secrets,
And never shows surprise,
He listens to my problems,
With kindness in his eyes.

And when I'm feeling lonely,
On him I can depend,
He's more than just a teddy,
He is my best, best friend!

SOME TEDDY BEARS

Some teddy bears are tiny,
Some teddy bears are tall,
Some teddy bears are big and round,
And some teddy bears are small.

Some teddy bears are woolly,
Some teddy bears are rough,
Some teddy bears have shaggy fur,
And some are balls of fluff.

Some teddy bears look happy
Some teddy bears look sad,
Some teddy bears are very good,
And some teddy bears are bad.

But all teddy bears are loyal,
And all teddy bears are true,
And all teddy bears need lots of love
And hugs from me and you.

WOBBLY BEAR

Mr and Mrs Puppety owned an old-fashioned toy shop. They made toys by hand in a room at the back of the shop. But they were getting old and their eyesight was bad.

"It's time we got an apprentice toymaker," said Mr Puppety to his wife. They soon found a young lad called Tom to work for them. He worked hard and carefully. He spent his first week making a teddy bear. When he had finished he showed the bear to Mr and Mrs Puppety.

"He looks very cuddly," said Mrs Puppety.

Tom was pleased that they liked his bear and he went off home whistling happily.

"He is a lovely bear," said Mr Puppety, "but his head is a bit wobbly."

"I know," said his wife, "but it's Tom's first try. Let's just put him up there on the shelf with the other teddy bears."

That night Wobbly Bear sat on the shelf and started to cry. He had heard what Mr and Mrs Puppety had said about him.

"What's wrong?" asked Brown Bear, who was sitting next to him.

"My head is on wobbly," sobbed Wonky Bear.

"Does it hurt?" asked Brown Bear.

"No," replied Wobbly Bear.

"Then why are you crying?" asked Brown Bear.

"Because nobody will want to buy a wobbly bear. I'll be left in this shop forever and nobody will ever take me home and love me," he cried.

"Don't worry," said Brown Bear. "We've all got our faults, and you look fine to me. Just try your best to look cute and cuddly and you'll soon have someone to love you." This made Wobbly Bear feel much happier and he soon fell fast asleep.

The next day the shop was full of people, but nobody paid any attention to Wobbly Bear. Then a little boy looked up at the shelf and cried, "Oh, what a lovely bear. Can I have that one, Daddy?"

Wobbly Bear's heart lifted as the little boy's daddy reached up to his shelf. But he picked up Brown Bear instead and handed him to the little boy. Wobbly Bear felt sadder than ever. Nobody wanted him. All of his new friends would get sold and leave the shop, but he would be left on the shelf gathering dust. Poor old Wobbly Bear!

Now, Mr and Mrs Puppety had a little grand-daughter called Jessie who loved to visit the shop and play with the toys. All the toys loved her because she was gentle and kind. It so happened that the next time she came to visit it was her birthday, and her grandparents told her she could choose any toy she wanted as her present.

"I know she won't choose me," thought Wobbly Bear sadly. "Not with all these other beautiful toys to choose from."

167

But to Wobbly amazement, Jessie looked up and pointed at his shelf and said, "I'd like that wobbly bear please. No one else will have a bear quite like him."

Mr Puppety smiled and gave Wobbly to Jessie. She hugged and kissed him, and Wobbly felt so happy he almost cried. She took him home and put a smart red bow around his neck ready for her birthday party. He felt very proud indeed.

Soon the other children arrived, each carrying their teddy bears under their arms.

Wobbly Bear could not believe his eyes when he saw the little boy with his friend Brown Bear!

"I'm having a teddy bears' picnic," Jessie explained to him, hugging him tight. All of the children and the bears had a wonderful time, especially Wobbly. He had found a lovely home, met his old friend and made lots of new ones.

"See, I told you not to worry," said Brown Bear.

"I know," said Wobbly. "And I never will again."

TEN LITTLE TEDDIES

Ten little teddies, standing in a line,
One of them went fishing, so then there were nine.

Nine little teddies, marching through a gate,
One stopped to tie his shoe, so then there were eight.

Eight little teddies, floating up in heaven,
One fell down and broke his crown,
so then there were seven.

Seven little teddies, doing magic tricks,
One made himself disappear, so then there were six.

Six little teddies, about to take a dive,
One of them was scared of heights, so then there were five.

Five little teddies, running on the shore,
One went surfing in the waves, so then there were four.

Four little teddies, eating cakes for tea,
One of them was feeling sick, so then there were three.

Three little teddies, heading for the zoo,
One of them hopped on a bus, so then there were two.

Two little teddies, playing in the sun,
One of them got sunburnt, so then there was one.

One little teddy, who's had lots of fun,
It's time for him to go to sleep, so now there are none.

BEARS AHOY

One summer's day, three little boys went for a picnic by the bank of a river. They took with them their swimming things, some cheese and tomato sandwiches and, of course, their teddy bears.

When they arrived, they found a small boat tied to a tree. The boys climbed on board, taking their teddies with them, and had a great game of pirates. The boys pretended to walk the plank, and soon they were all splashing about, playing and swimming in the river. They chased each other through the shallow water, and disappeared along the river and out of sight.

Now, the three bears left on board the boat did not get on very well together. Oscar was a small, honey-colored bear. He was good friends with Mabel, who had shaggy brown fur, but neither of them liked Toby. He was bigger than they were and he was a bully. He was always growling at the other bears and telling them what to do.

As soon as the boys were out of sight, Toby leapt to his feet. The boat rocked. Oscar and Mabel begged him to sit down.

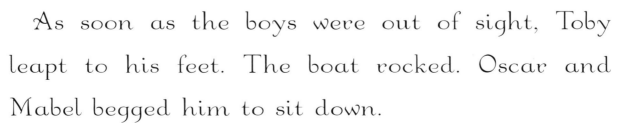

"I'm a fearless sailor," cried Toby. "I've sailed the seven seas and now I'm going to sail them again." He untied the boat, and pushed it away from the bank. The boat lurched from side to side.

"Come on, crew. Look lively!" shouted Toby. "Do as I say or I'll make you walk the plank." Now that it was untied, the little blue boat began to drift. It turned sideways gently, then caught the main current and began to gather speed.

174

Toby!" cried Oscar. "We're moving!"

"Of course we are, you big softie," growled Toby. "We're bold and fearless pirates on the high seas."

Oscar and Mabel clung together in fright, as the little boat sailed down the river, past fields and houses. "Help!" they shouted. "Toby, make it stop!" But Toby was having a great time.

"Ha, ha," shouted Toby. "This is the life!"

Oscar glanced over the side. He wished he hadn't. The sight of everything passing by so quickly made him feel seasick.

"Look out, Toby!" he cried. "We're going to hit the bank. Steer it away."

But Toby did nothing. The boat hit the bank with a thump and Toby fell forward. The boat swung round and headed for the middle of the river once more.

"Toby!" shouted Mabel. "Save us!"

But Toby was sitting in the bottom of the boat, rubbing a big bump on his head.

"I can't. I don't know how to sail a boat," he whimpered, feebly. He hid his face in his paws and began to cry. The boat zig-zagged on down the river, with the little bears clinging on to the sides in fright. In time, the river became wider and they could hear the cry of seagulls.

"Oh, Toby," cried Mabel. "We're heading for the sea. Do something!"

"Nobody likes me," wailed Toby. "Now we're going to sink to the bottom of the sea, and you won't like me either!"

Oscar wasn't listening. He had found a rope hanging from the sail. "Let's put the sail up and see if it will blow us to shore," he said.

"We'll be blown out to sea," wailed Toby, but Oscar ignored him, and carried on. The wind filled the sail and the little boat started moving forward. They sailed right across the bay to the far side, and blew up on to the beach.

"Oh, Oscar, you are a hero!" sighed Mabel, hugging him tight. "You saved us!"

Imagine the bears' surprise to see the three little boys running towards them along the beach — they had gone to find the coastguard and raise the alarm. There were hugs and kisses all round when they found the bears safe and sound. And you can be sure that from that day on, Toby was a much wiser and kinder bear, and he never bullied the others again.

TEDDY BEAR TEARS

"Boo hoo! I want to go home!"

As a little fairy called Mavis flew past the garbage dump, holding her nose, she heard an unmistakeable sound coming from the other side of a very smelly pile of garbage.

"Oh, dear. Those sound like teddy bear tears," she said to herself. "I'd better go and see if I can help."

She flew down to take a look, and sure enough, there amongst a heap of old potato peelings and banana skins sat a very old, very sad teddy indeed. Mavis sat and held his paw, while he told her what had happened:

"My owner, Matylda, was told to clean out her room. She's terribly messy, but she's sweet and kind," Teddy sniffed. "She threw me out with an old blanket by mistake — she didn't realise I was tucked up having a sleep inside it. Then some

men in a big dirty truck came and emptied me out of the trash can and brought me here. But I want to go home!" And with that poor Teddy started to cry again.

"There, there," said Mavis. "I'll help to get you home. But first I'll need two teddy bear tears." She unscrewed the lid of a little jar, and scooped two big salty tears into it from Teddy's cheeks.

"What do you need those for?" asked Teddy; feeling rather bewildered.

"Just a little fairy magic!" said Mavis. "Now wait here, and I promise I'll be back soon." And with a wave of her wand she disappeared.

Teddy pulled the blanket around him, and sat trying to be brave, and not to cry. He stayed like that all night, feeling cold and alone and frightened. How he wished he was back in his warm cozy home.

Meanwhile Mavis was very busy. She flew back and forth around the neighborhood, until she heard the sound of sobbing coming from an open window. She flew down onto the window sill and peered inside. A little girl was lying on the bed, with her mommy sitting beside her.

"I want my teddy!" she cried.

"Well if you weren't so messy Matylda, you wouldn't lose things," said Mommy gently.

"But I cleaned my room today!" said Matylda.

"Well, try and go to sleep now," said Mommy, kissing her goodnight, "and we'll look for Teddy in the morning."

Mavis watched as poor Matylda lay sobbing into her pillow, until at last she fell fast asleep. Then Mavis flew down from the window sill, took out the little jar, and rubbed Teddy's tears onto Matylda's sleeping eyes. With a little fizzle of stars, the fairy magic began to work, and Matylda started to dream. She could see an old tire, a newspaper, some tin cans, some orange

peel, a blanket... wait a minute, it was her blanket, and there, wrapped inside it was her teddy, with a big tear running down his cheek! Teddy was at the garbage dump!

The next morning, Matylda woke with a start, and remembered her dream at once. She ran downstairs to the kitchen, where Mommy was making breakfast, and told her all about it.

"We have to go to the garbage dump! We have to save Teddy!" said Matylda.

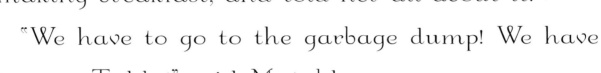

Mommy tried to explain that it was just a dream, but Matylda wouldn't listen, so in the end they set off to take a look.

They arrived just as a big machine was scooping up the garbage and heading for the crusher. And there, on top of the scoop, clinging to the edge, was Teddy!

Mavis appeared, hovering in the air above him. "Don't worry, we'll save you!" she said. She waved her wand in a bright flash above Teddy. Matylda looked up and spotted him at once.

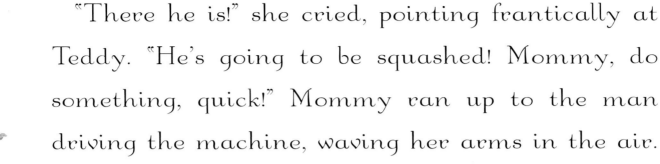

"There he is!" she cried, pointing frantically at Teddy. "He's going to be squashed! Mommy, do something, quick!" Mommy ran up to the man driving the machine, waving her arms in the air.

He stopped his machine just in time.

Soon Teddy and Matylda were reunited, and there were more tears, although this time they were happy ones. And from then on, Matylda's room was the tidiest room you have ever seen.

MIDNIGHT FUN

Just as midnight's striking,
When everyone's asleep,
Teddies yawn and stretch and shake,
And out of warm beds creep.

They sneak out from their houses,
And gather in the dark,
Then skip along the empty streets,
Heading for the park.

And there beneath the moonlight,
They tumble down the slides,
They swoosh up high upon the swings,
And play on all the rides.

And when the sun comes peeping,
They rush home to their beds,
And snuggle down as children wake,
To cuddle with their teds!

POOR LITTLE TED

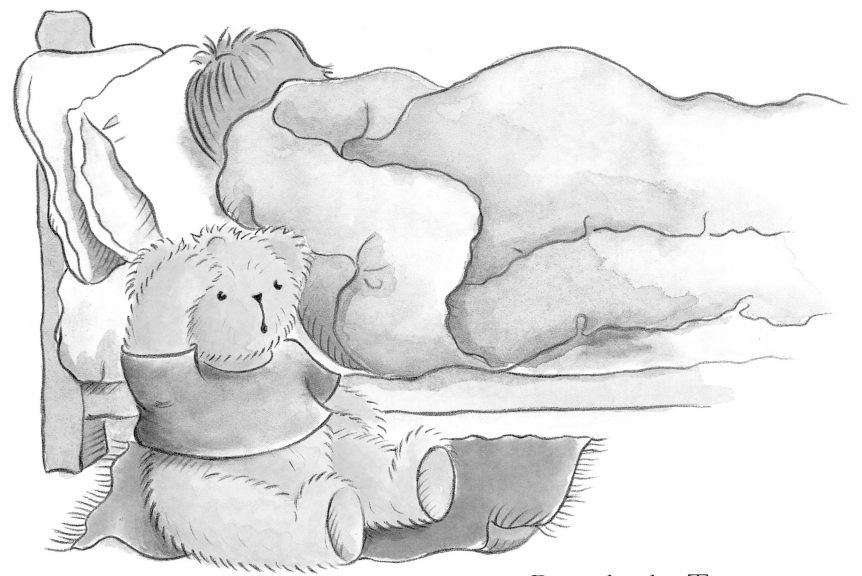

Poor little Ted
Fell out of bed,
And found that he had
A big bump on his head!

He let out a scream,
I woke from my dream,
And soon made him better
With cake and ice-cream!

IN A SPIN

I had a little teddy,
He went everywhere with me,
But now I've gone and lost him,
Oh, where can my teddy be?

I've looked behind the sofa,
I've looked beneath the bed,
I've looked out in the garden,
And in the garden shed!

I've looked inside the bathtub,
And underneath my chair,
Oh, where, oh, where is Teddy?
I've hunted everywhere!

At last I try the kitchen,
My face breaks in a grin.
There's Teddy in the washtub –
Mom's sent him for a spin!

Illustrations by:
Georgie Birkett, Stephanie Boey, Mario Capaldi,
Dorothy Clark, Kate Davies, Maggie Downer, Frank Endersby,
Serena Feneziani, Andrew Geeson, Piers Harper, Elaine Keary,
Angela Kincaid, Jane Molineaux, Claire Mumford, Rikki O'Neill,
Pauline Siewart, Jessica Stockham and Linda Worrell.